W9-AUS-914

A RAILWAY ABC

BY JACK TOWNEND

V&A Publishing

First published in 1942
This edition published by
V&A Publishing, 2015

V&A Publishing
Victoria and Albert Museum
South Kensington
London SW7 2RL
www.vandapublishing.com

Distributed in North America by
Abrams Books for Yound Readers,
an imprint of ABRAMS

© 2015 Estate of Jack Townend

Jack Townend (1918–2005) was an English artist and illustrator. *A Railway ABC* is in the collection of the Victoria and Albert Museum's National Art Library, which includes over 100,000 children's books.

ISBN 978 1 85177 844 7

Library of Congress Control Number
2014946846

10 9 8 7 6 5 4 3 2 1
2018 2017 2016 2015

A catalogue record for this book is
available from the British Library.

All rights reserved. No part of this
publication may be reproduced, stored
in a retrieval system, or transmitted in
any form or by any means electronic,
mechanical, photocopying, recording or
otherwise, without the written permission
of the publishers.

Printed in China

V&A Publishing

Supporting the world's leading
museum of art and design,
the Victoria and Albert
Museum, London

FOR
BETTY

for
ALL CLEAR
as the
signal goes
down

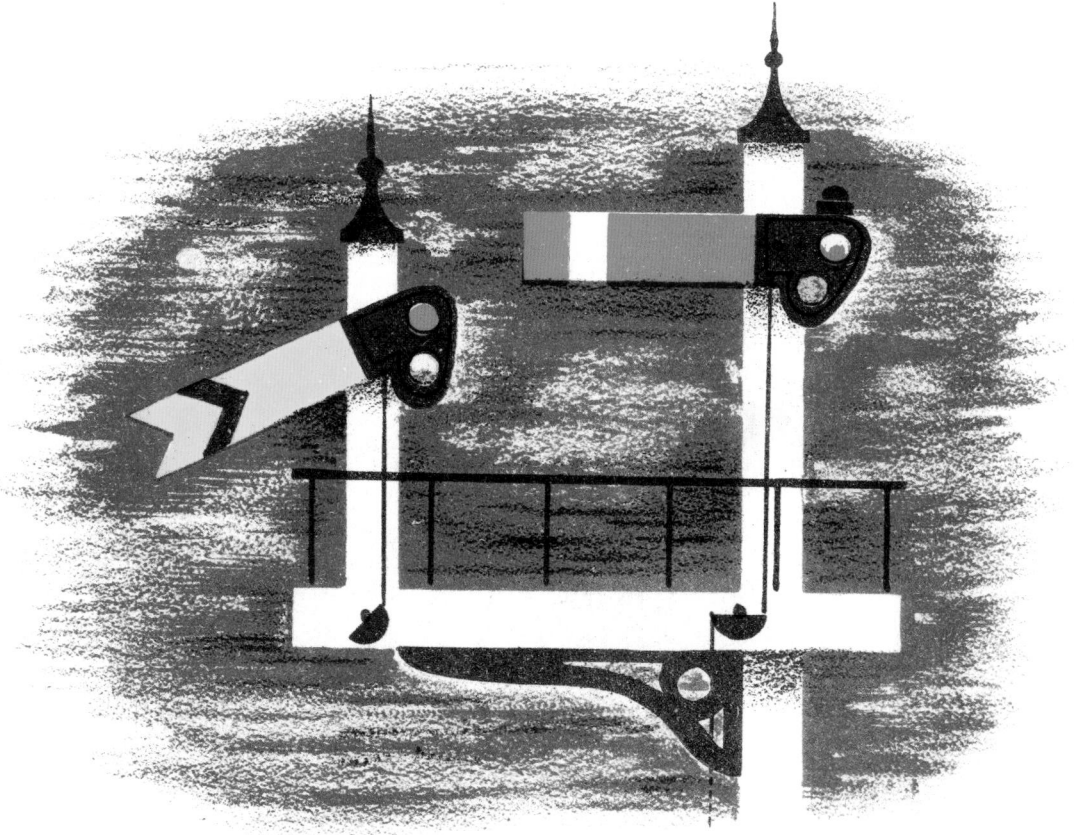

B

for the
BUFFERS
which sit
there
and frown

for the
COACHES
in which
we all
ride

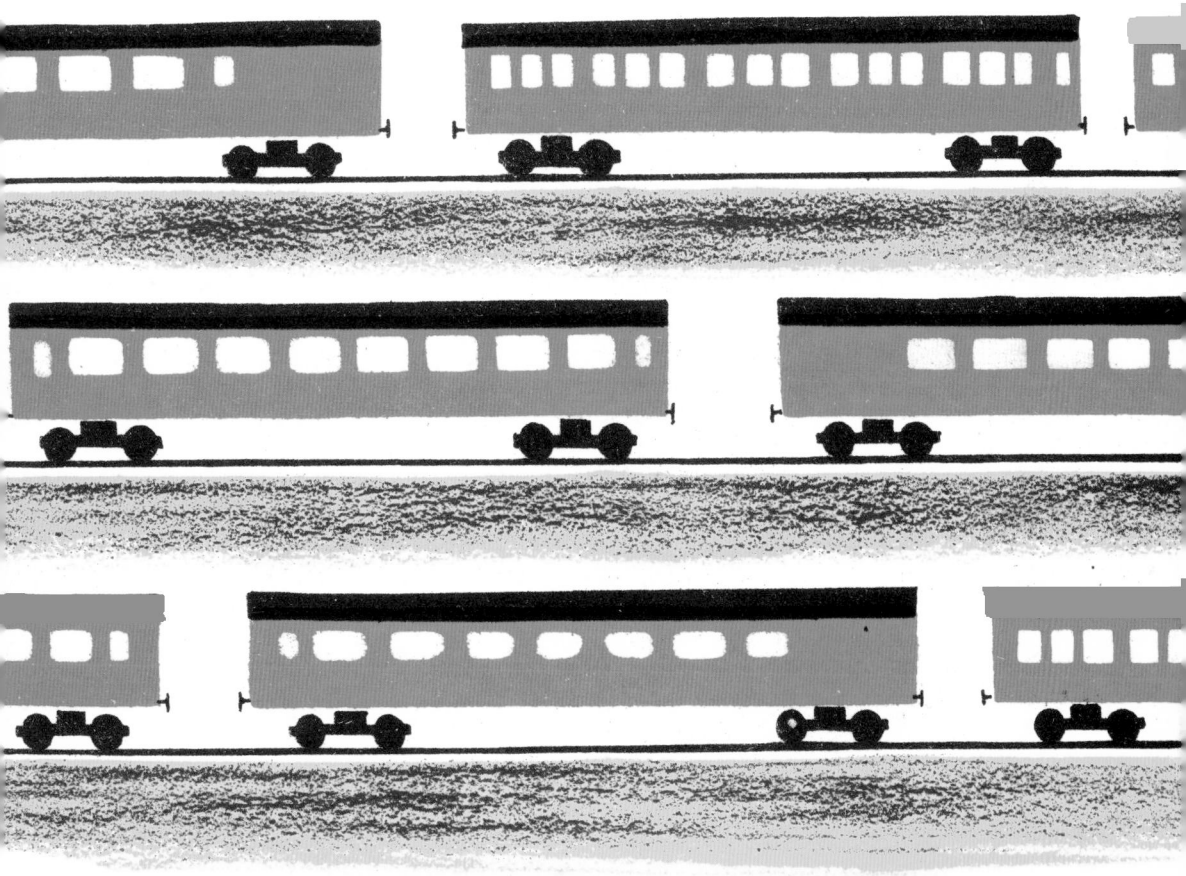

for the
DRIVER
the engine's
his pride

is an

ENGINE

spick

and

span

for the
FIREMAN
whose
name
is Dan

for the
GUARD
as his
whistle
he blows

GUARD

is the
HOPPER
through which
the coal
goes

the INSPECTOR who stands at the gate

for the
JUNCTION
here's
where
we wait

JUNCTION

for the
KITCHEN
with pans
all
a-glow

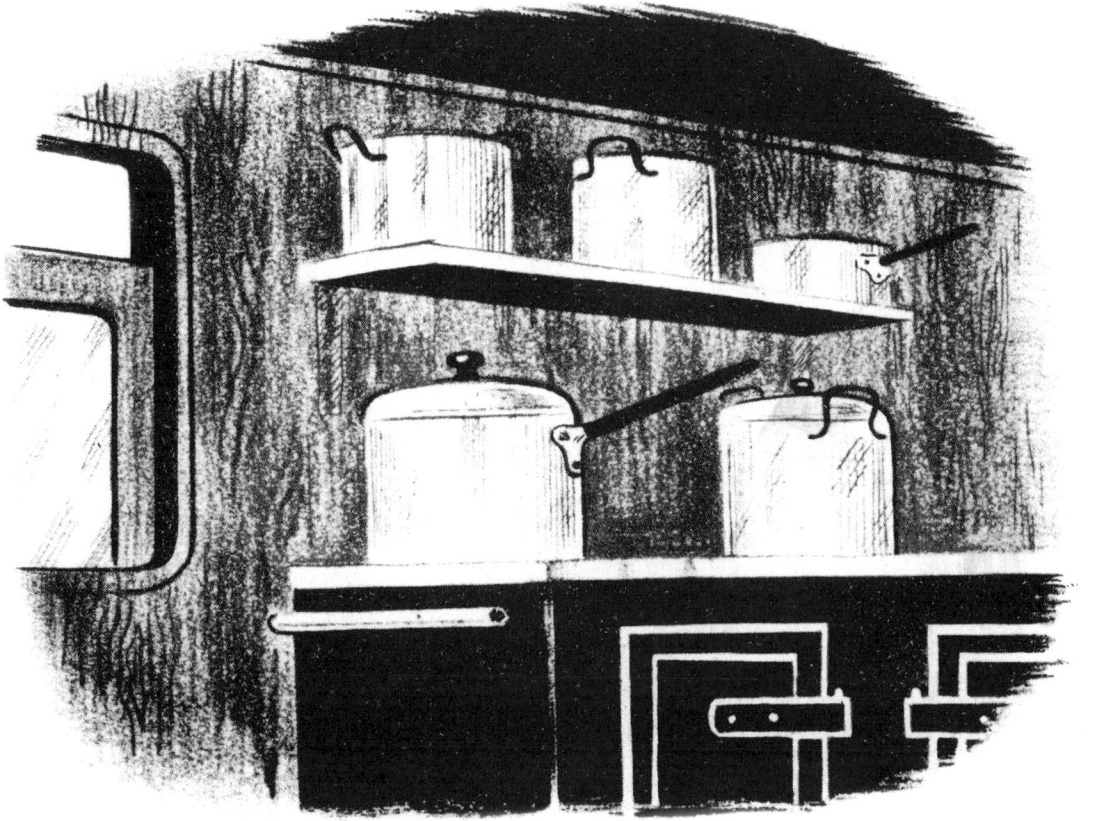

for the
LAMPS
which
stand in
a row

is the
MAIL
which is
urgent
indeed

G R

is a

NIGHT-TRAIN

running

at

speed

is the
OLD MAN
who
works on
the line

for the
PORTER
he's
sturdy
and fine

3

is the
QUEUE
for the
train which
is late

for the
RAILS
some curved
and
some straight

for the
SIGNALS
which say
"Stop"
or "Go"

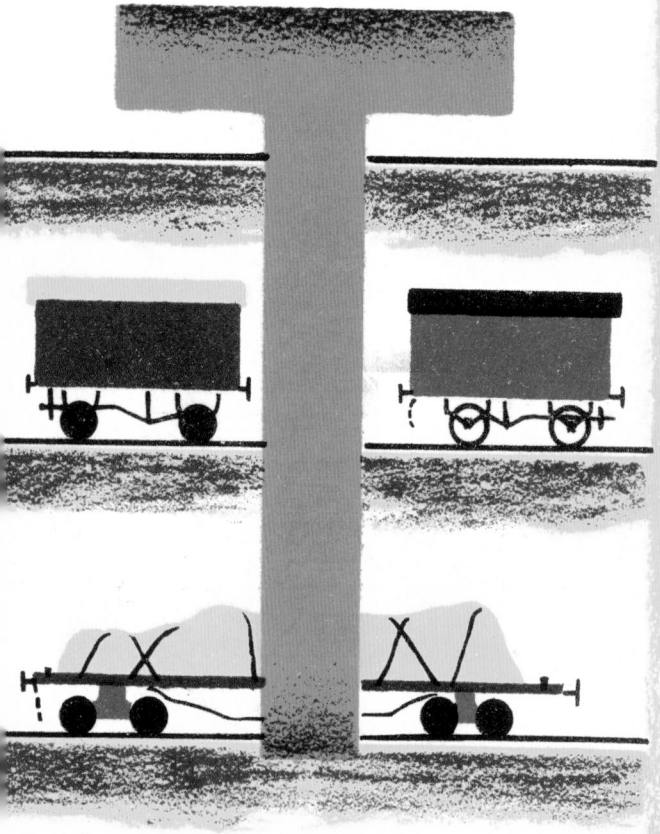

for the
TRUCKS
some high
and
some low

BRICKS
GUARD
FRUIT
COAL

the
UMBRELLA
left
by
Aunt Sally

is the
VIADUCT
which
crosses
the valley

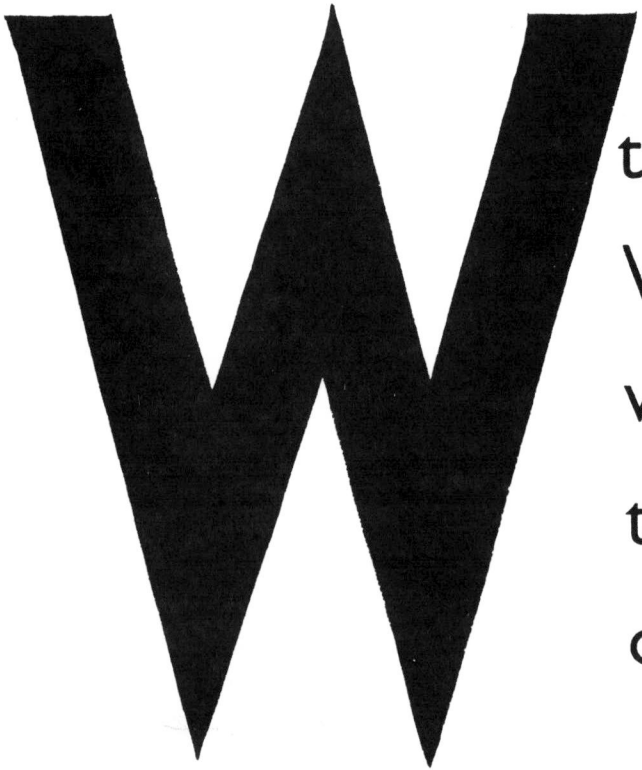

the

WATER-TANK

where

the engines

drink

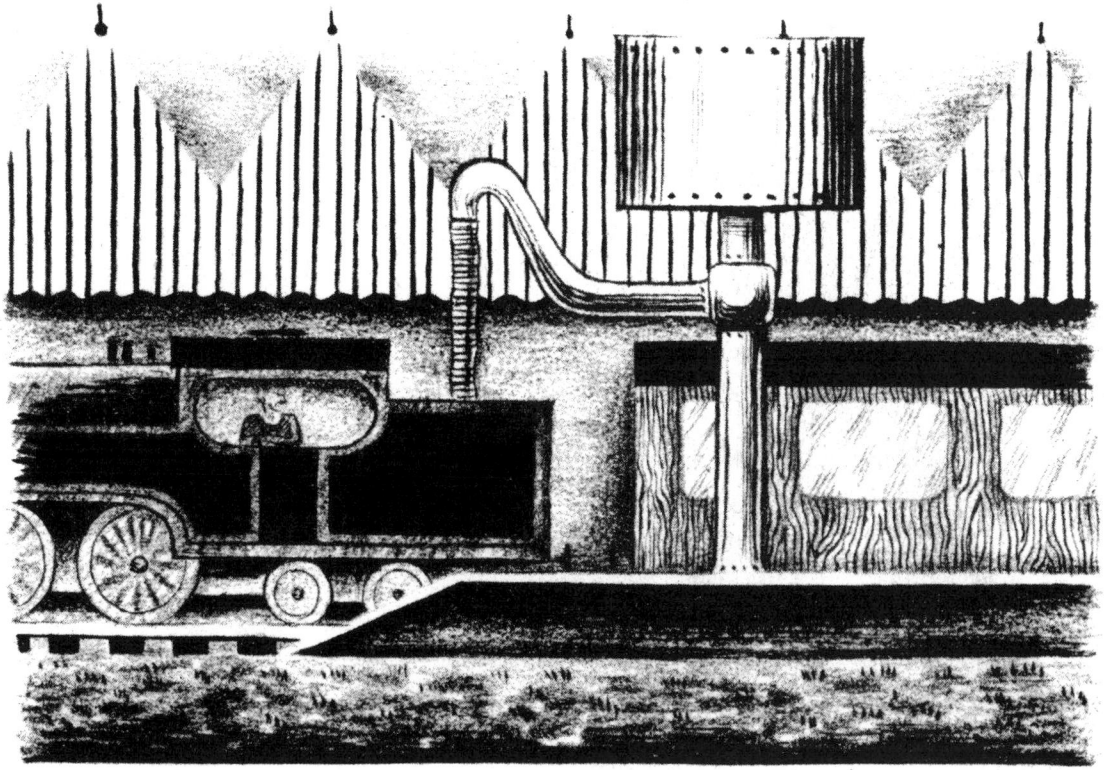

is the
CROSSING
where the
red light
blinks

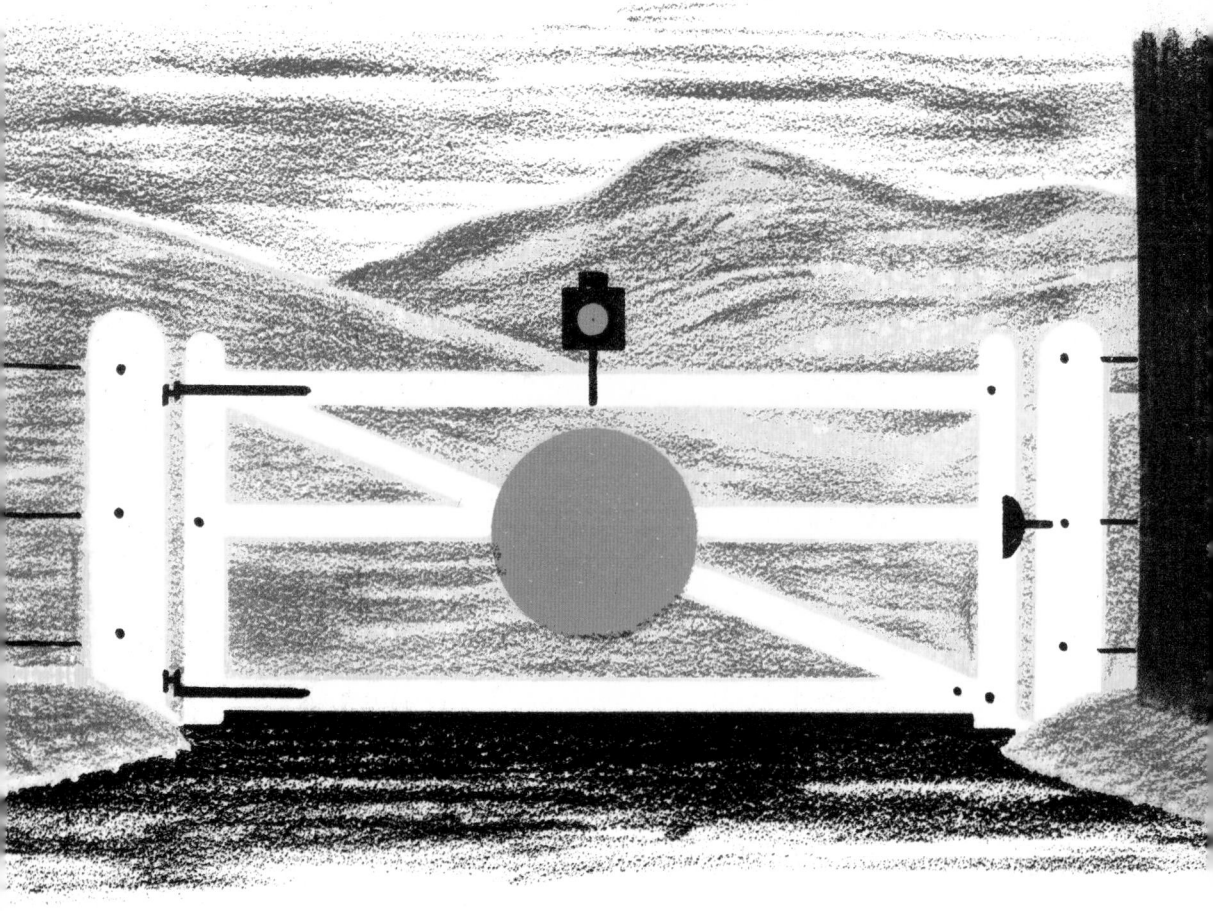

is for
YORK
a very
big
Station

YORK

is the
ZOO
which
is our
destination

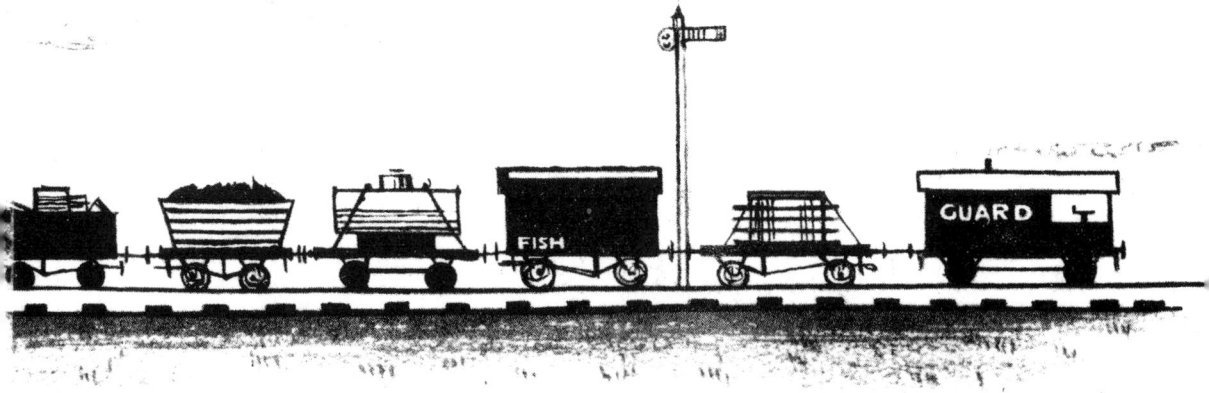
FISH
GUARD

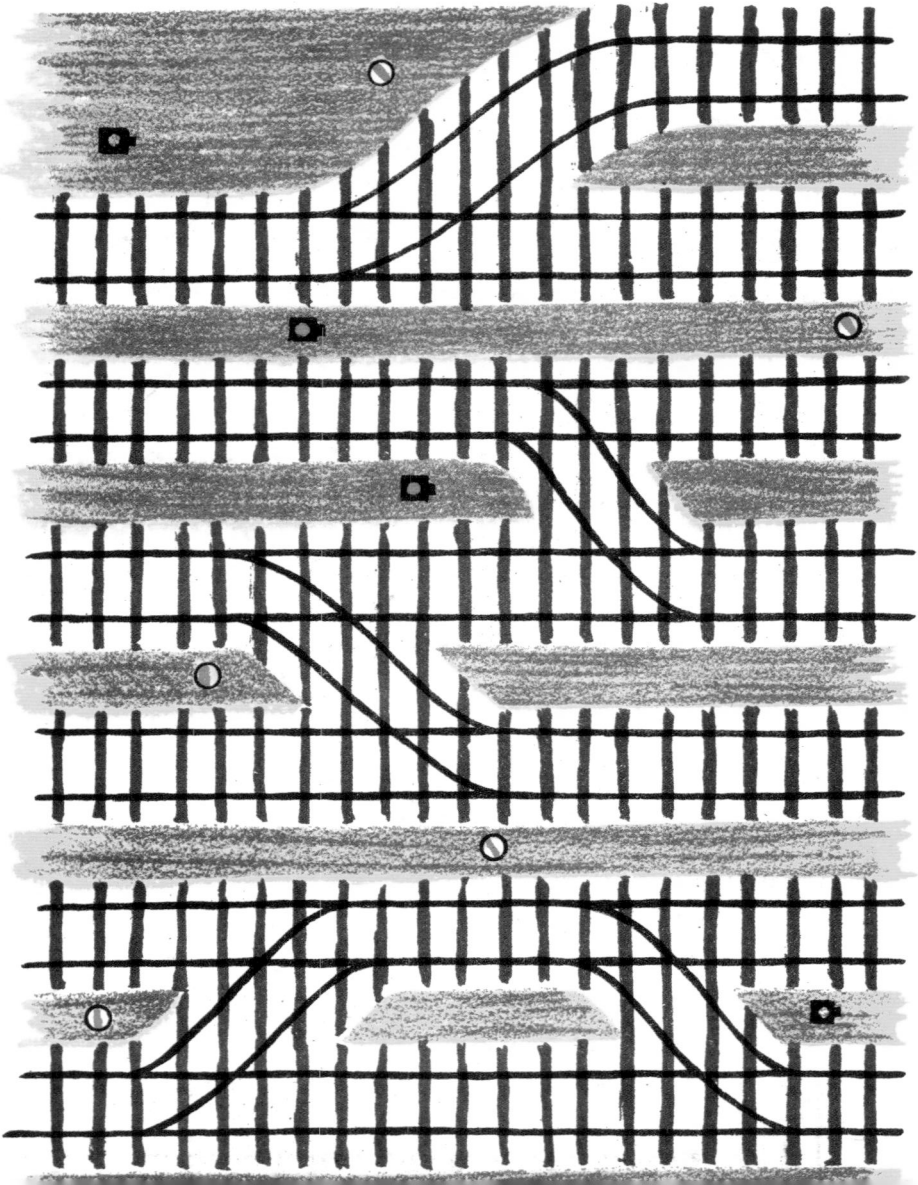